The Mines of Falun

By

E. T. A. Hoffmann

British Library Cataloguing-in-Publication Data
A catalogue record for this book is available from the
British Library

E. T. A. Hoffman

Ernst Theodor Wilhelm Hoffmann was born in Königsberg, East Prussia in 1776. His family were all jurists, and during his youth he was initially encouraged to pursue a career in law. However, in his late teens Hoffman became increasingly interested in literature and philosophy, and spent much of his time reading German classicists and attending lectures by, amongst others, Immanuel Kant.

In was in his twenties, upon moving with his uncle to Berlin, that Hoffman first began to promote himself as a composer, writing an operetta called Die Maske and entering a number of playwriting competitions. Hoffman struggled to establish himself anywhere for a while, flitting between a number of cities and dodging the attentions of Napoleon's occupying troops. In 1808, while living in Bamberg, he began his job as a theatre manager and a music critic, and Hoffman's break came a year later, with the publication of Ritter Gluck. The story centred on a man who meets, or thinks he has met, a long-dead composer, and played into the 'doppelgänger' theme – at that time very popular in literature. It was shortly after this that Hoffman began to use the pseudonym E. T. A. Hoffmann, declaring the 'A' to stand for 'Amadeus', as a tribute to the great composer, Mozart.

Over the next decade, while moving between Dresden, Leipzig and Berlin, Hoffman produced a great range of both literary and musical works. Probably Hoffman's most well-known story, produced in 1816, is 'The Nutcracker and the Mouse King', due to the fact that – some seventy-six years later - it inspired Tchaikovsky's ballet The Nutcracker.

In the same vein, his story 'The Sandman' provided both the inspiration for Léo Delibes's ballet Coppélia, and the basis for a highly influential essay by Sigmund Freud, called 'The Uncanny'. (Indeed, Freud referred to Hoffman as the "unrivalled master of the uncanny in literature.")

Alcohol abuse and syphilis eventually took a great toll on Hoffman though, and – having spent the last year of his life paralysed – he died in Berlin in 1822, aged just 46. His legacy is a powerful one, however: He is seen as a pioneer of both Romanticism and fantasy literature, and his novella, Mademoiselle de Scudéri: A Tale from the Times of Louis XIV is often cited as the first ever detective story.

The Mines of Falun

"**One** bright, sunny day in July the whole population of Goethaborg was assembled at the harbour. A fine East-Indiaman, happily returned from her long voyage, was lying at anchor, with her long, homeward-bound pennant, and the Swedish flag fluttering gaily in the azure sky. Hundreds of boats, skiffs, and other small craft, thronged with rejoicing seafolk, were going to and fro on the mirroring waters of the Goethaelf, and the cannon of Masthuggetorg thundered their far-echoing greeting out to sea. The gentlemen of the East-India Company were walking up and down on the quay, reckoning up, with smiling faces, the plentiful profits they had netted, and rejoicing their hearts at the yearly increasing success of their hazardous enterprise, and at the growing commercial importance of their good town of Goethaborg. For the same reasons everybody looked at these brave adventurers with pleasure and pride, and shared their rejoicing; for their success brought sap and vigour into the whole life of the place.

"The crew of the East-Indiaman, about a hundred strong, landed in a number of boats (gaily dressed with flags for the occasion) and prepared to hold their 'Hoensning.' That is the name of the feast which the sailors hold on such occasions; it often goes on for several days. Musicians went before them, in strange, gay dresses, playing lustily on violins, oboes, fifes and drums, whilst others sung merry songs; after them came the crew, walking two and two; some, with gay ribbons on

7

The Mines of Falun

their hats and jackets, waved fluttering streamers; others danced and skipped; and all of them shouted and cheered at the tops of their voices, till the sounds of merriment rang far and wide.

"Thus the gay procession passed through the streets, and on to the Haga suburb, where a feast of eating and drinking was ready for them in a tavern.

"Here the best of 'Oel' flowed in rivers and bumper after bumper was quaffed. Numbers of women joined them, as is always the case when sailors come home from a long voyage; dancing began, and wilder and wilder grew the revel, and louder and louder the din.

"One sailor only--a slender, handsome lad of about twenty, or scarcely so much--had slipped away from the revel, and was sitting alone outside, on the bench at the door of the tavern.

"Two or three of his shipmates came out to him, and cried, laughing loudly:

"'Now then, Elis Froebom! are you going to be a donkey, as usual, and sit out here in the sulks, instead of joining the sport like a man? Why, you might as well part company from the old ship altogether, and set sail on your own hook, as fight shy of the "Hoensning." One would think you were a regular long-shore land-lubber, and had never been afloat on blue water. All the same, you've got as good pluck as any sailor that walks a deck--ay, and as cool and steady a head in a gale of wind as ever I came athwart; but, you see, you can't take your liquor! You'd sooner keep the ducats in your pocket than serve them out to the land-sharks ashore here. There, lad! take a drink of that; or Naecken, the sea-devil, and all the Troll will be foul of your hawse before you know where you are!'

"Elis Froebom jumped up quickly from the bench; glared angrily at his shipmates; took the tumbler--which was filled to the brim with brandy--and emptied it at a draught; then he said:

"'You see I can take my glass with any man of you, Ivens; and you can ask the captain if I'm a good sailor-man, or not; so stow away that long tongue of yours, and sheer off! I don't care about all this drink and row here; and what I'm doing out here by myself is no business of yours; you have nothing to do with it.'

"'All right, my hearty!' answered Ivens. 'I know all about it. You're one of these Nerica men--and a moony lot the whole cargo of them are too. They're the sort of chaps that would rather sit and pipe their eye about nothing particular, than take a good glass, and see what the pretty lasses at home are made of, after a twelve-month's cruize! But just you belay there a bit. Steer full and bye, and stand off and on, and I'll send somebody out to you that'll cut you adrift, in a pig's whisper, from that old bench where you've cast your anchor.'

"They went; and presently a very pretty, rather refined-looking girl came out of the tavern, and sat down beside the melancholy Elis, who was still sitting, silent and thoughtful, on the bench. From her dress and general appearance there could be no doubt as to her terrible calling. But the life she

9

was leading had not yet quite marred the delicacy of the wonderfully tender features of her beautiful face; there was no trace of repulsive boldness about the expression of her dark eyes--rather a quiet, melancholy longing.

"'Aren't you coming to join your shipmates, Elis?' she said. 'Now that you're back safe and sound, after all you've gone through on your long voyage, aren't you glad to be home in the old country again?'

"The girl spoke in a soft, gentle voice, putting her arms about him. Elis Froebom looked into her eyes, as if roused from a dream. He took her hand; he pressed her to his breast. It was evident that what she had said had made its way to his heart.

"'Ah!' he said, as if collecting his thoughts, 'it's no use talking about my enjoying myself. I can't join in all that riot and uproar; there's no pleasure in it, for me. You go away, my dear child! Sing and shout like the rest of them, if you can, and let the gloomy, melancholy Elis stay out here by himself; he would only spoil your pleasure. Wait a minute, though! I like you, and I should wish you to think of me sometimes, when I'm away on the sea again.'

"With that he took two shining ducats out of his pocket, and a beautiful Indian handkerchief from his breast, and gave them to the girl. But her eyes streamed with tears; she rose, laid the money on the bench, and said:

"'Oh, keep your ducats; they only make me miserable; but I'll wear the handkerchief in dear remembrance of you. You're not likely to find me next year when you hold your

10

Hoensning in the Haga.'

"And she crept slowly away down the street, with her hands pressed to her face.

"Elis fell back into his gloomy reveries. At length, as the uproar in the tavern grew loud and wild, he cried:

"'Oh, that I were lying deep, deep beneath the sea! for there's nobody left in the wide, wide world that I can be happy with now!'

"A deep, harsh voice spoke, close behind him: 'You must have been most unfortunate, youngster, to wish to die, just when life should be opening before you.'

"Elis looked round, and saw an old miner standing leaning against the boarded wall of the tavern, with folded arms, looking down at him with a grave, penetrating glance.

"As Elis looked at him, a feeling came to him as if some familiar figure had suddenly come into the deep, wild solitude in which he had thought himself lost. He pulled himself together, and told the old miner that his father had been a stout sailor, but had perished in the storm from which he himself had been saved as by a miracle; that his two soldier brothers had died in battle, and he had supported his mother with the liberal pay he drew for sailing to the East Indies. He said he had been obliged to follow the life of a sailor, having been brought up to it from childhood, and it had been a great piece of good fortune that he got into the service of the East-India Company. This voyage, the profits had been greater than usual, and each of the crew had been given a sum of money over and above his pay; so that he had hastened, in the highest spirits, with his pockets full of ducats, to the little cottage where his mother lived. But strange faces looked at him from the windows, and a young woman who opened the door to him at last told him, in a cold, harsh tone, that his mother had died three months before, and that he would find the few bits of things that were left, after paying the funeral expenses, waiting for him at the Town Hall. The death of his mother broke his heart. He felt alone in the world--as much so as if he had been wrecked on some lonely reef, helpless and miserable. All his life at sea seemed to him to have been a mistaken, purposeless driving. And when he thought of his mother, perhaps badly looked after by strangers, he thought it a wrong and horrible thing that he should have gone to sea at all, instead of staying at home and taking proper care of her. His comrades had dragged him to the Hoensning in spite of himself, and he had thought, too, that the uproar, and even the drink, might have deadened his pain; but instead of that, all the veins in his breast seemed to be bursting, and he felt as if he must bleed to death.

"'Well,' said the old miner, 'you'll soon be off to sea again, Elis, and then your sorrow will soon be over. Old folks must die; there's no help for that: she has only gone from this miserable world to a better.'

"Ah!' said Elis, 'it is just because nobody believes in my sorrow, and that they all think me a fool to feel it--I say it's that which is driving me out of the world! I shan't go to sea any more; I'm sick of existence altogether. When the ship used to go flying along through the water, with all sail set, spreading like glorious wings, the waves playing and dashing in exquisite music, and the wind singing in the rigging, my heart used to bound. Then I could hurrah and shout on deck like the best of them. And when I was on look-out duty of dark, quiet nights, I used to think about getting home, and how glad my dear old mother would be to have me back. I could enjoy a Hoensning like the rest of them, then. And when I had shaken the ducats into mother's lap, and given her the handkerchiefs and all the other pretty things I had brought home, her eyes would sparkle with pleasure, and she would clap her hands for joy, and run out and in, and fetch me the "Aehl" which she had kept for my homecoming. And when I sat with her of an evening, I would tell her of all the strange folks I had seen, and their ways and customs, and about the wonderful things I had come across in my long voyages. This delighted her; and she would tell me of my father's wonderful cruizes in the far North, and serve me up lots of strange, sailor's yarns, which I had heard a hundred times, but never could hear too often. Ah! who will give me that happiness back again? No, no! never more on land!-- never more at sea! What should I do among my shipmates? They would only laugh at me. Where should I find any heart for my work? It would be nothing but an objectless striving.'

"It gives me real satisfaction to listen to you, youngster,' said the old miner. 'I have been observing you, without your knowledge, for the last hour or two, and have had my own enjoyment in so doing. All that you have said and done has shown me that you possess a profoundly thoughtful mind, and a character and nature pious, simple, and sincere. Heaven could have given you no more precious gifts; but you were never in all your born days in the least cut out for a sailor. How should the wild, unsettled sailor's life suit a meditative, melancholy Neriker like you?--for I can see that you come from Nerica by your features, and whole appearance. You are right to say good-bye to that life for ever. But you're not going to walk about idle, with your hands in your pockets? Take my advice, Elis Froebom. Go to Falun, and be a miner. You are young and strong. You'll soon be a first-class pick-hand; then a hewer; presently a surveyor, and so get higher and higher. You have a lot of ducats in your pocket. Take care of them; invest them; add more to them. Very likely you'll soon get a "Hemmans" of your own, and then a share in the works. Take my advice, Elis Froebom; be a miner.'

"The old man's words caused him a sort of fear.

"'What?' he cried. 'Would you have me leave the bright, sunny sky that revives and refreshes me, and go down into that dreadful, hell-like abyss, and dig and tunnel like a mole for metals and ores, merely to gain a few wretched ducats? Oh, never!'

"'The usual thing,' said the old man. 'People despise what they have had no chance of knowing anything about! As if all the constant wearing, petty anxieties inseparable from business up here on the surface, were nobler than the miner's work. To his skill, knowledge, and untiring industry Nature lays bare her most secret treasures. You speak of gain with contempt, Elis Froebom. Well, there's something infinitely

14

higher in question here, perhaps: the mole tunnels the ground from blind instinct; but, it may be, in the deepest depths, by the pale glimmer of the mine candle, men's eyes get to see clearer, and at length, growing stronger and stronger, acquire the power of reading in the stones, the gems, and the minerals, the mirroring of secrets which are hidden above the clouds. You know nothing about mining, Elis. Let me tell you a little.'

"He sat down on the bench beside Elis, and began to describe the various processes minutely, placing all the details before him in the clearest and brightest colours. He talked of the Mines of Falun, in which he said he had worked since he was a boy; he described the great main-shaft, with its dark brown sides; he told how incalculably rich the mine was in gems of the finest water. More and more vivid grew his words, more and more glowing his face. He went, in his description, through the different shafts as if they had been the alleys of some enchanted garden. The jewels came to life, the fossils began to move; the wondrous Pyrosmalite and the Almandine flashed in the light of the miner's candles; the Rock-Crystals glittered, and darted their rays.

"Elis listened intently. The old man's strange way of speaking of all these subterranean marvels as if he were standing in the midst of them, impressed him deeply. His breast felt stifled; it seemed to him as if he were already down in these depths with the old man, and would never more look upon the friendly light of day. And yet it seemed as though the old man were opening to him a new and unknown world, to

15

which he really properly belonged, and that he had somehow felt all the magic of that world, in mystic forebodings, since his boyhood.

"Elis Froebom,' said the old man at length, 'I have laid before you all the glories of a calling for which Nature really destined you. Think the subject well over with yourself, and then act as your better judgment counsels you.'

"He rose quickly from the bench, and strode away without any good-bye to Elis, without looking at him even. Soon he disappeared from his sight.

"Meanwhile quietness had set in in the tavern. The strong 'Aehl' and brandy had got the upper hand. Many of the sailors had gone away with the girls; others were lying snoring in corners. Elis--who could go no more to his old home--asked for, and was given, a little room to sleep in.

"Scarcely had he thrown himself, worn and weary as he was, upon his bed, when dreams began to wave their pinions over him. He thought he was sailing in a beautiful vessel on a sea calm and clear as a mirror, with a dark, cloudy sky vaulted overhead. But when he looked down into the sea he presently saw that what he had thought was water was a firm, transparent, sparkling substance, in the shimmer of which the ship, in a wonderful manner, melted away, so that he found himself standing upon this floor of crystal, with a vault of black rock above him, for that was rock which he had taken at first for clouds. Impelled by some power unknown to him he stepped onwards, but, at that moment, every thing around him began to move, and wonderful plants and flowers, of

16

glittering metal, came shooting up out of the crystal mass he was standing on, and entwined their leaves and blossoms in the loveliest manner. The crystal floor was so transparent that Elis could distinctly see the roots of these plants. But soon, as his glance penetrated deeper and deeper, he saw, far, far down in the depths, innumerable beautiful maidens, holding each other embraced with white, gleaming arms; and it was from their hearts that the roots, plants, and flowers were growing. And when these maidens smiled, a sweet sound rang all through the vault above, and the wonderful metal-flowers shot up higher, and waved their leaves and branches in joy. An indescribable sense of rapture came upon the lad; a world of love and passionate longing awoke in his heart.

"'Down, down to you!' he cried, and threw himself with outstretched arras down upon the crystal ground. But it gave way under him, and he seemed to be floating in shimmering æther.

"'Ha! Elis Froebom; what think you of this world of glory?' a strong voice cried. It was the old miner. But as Elis looked at him, he seemed to expand into gigantic size, and to be made of glowing metal. Elis was beginning to be terrified; but a brilliant light came darting, like a sudden lightning-flash, out of the depths of the abyss, and the earnest face of a grand, majestic woman appeared. Elis felt the rapture of his heart swelling and swelling into destroying pain. The old man had hold of him, and cried:

"'Take care, Elis Froebom! That is the queen. You may look up now.'

"He turned his head involuntarily, and saw the stars of the night sky shining through a cleft in the vault overhead. A gentle voice called his name as if in inconsolable sorrow. It was his mother's. He thought he saw her form up at the cleft. But it was a young and beautiful woman who was calling him, and stretching her hands down into the vault.

"'Take me up!' he cried to the old man. I tell you I belong to the upper world, and its familiar, friendly sky.'

"'Take care, Froebom,' said the old man solemnly; 'be faithful to the queen, whom you have devoted yourself to.'

"But now, when he looked down again into the immobile face of the majestic woman, he felt that his personality dissolved away into glowing molten stone. He screamed aloud, in nameless fear, and awoke from this dream of wonder, whose rapture and terror echoed deep within his being.

"'I suppose I could scarcely help dreaming all this extraordinary stuff,' he said to himself, as he collected his senses with difficulty; 'the old miner told me so much about the glories of the subterranean world that of course my head's quite full of it. But I never in my life felt as I do now. Perhaps I'm dreaming still. No, no; I suppose I must be a little out of sorts. Let's get into the open air. The fresh sea-breeze'll soon set me all right.'

"He pulled himself together, and ran to the Klippa Haven, where the uproar of the Hoensning was breaking out again. But he soon found that all enjoyment passed him by, that he couldn't hold any thought fast in his mind, that presages and wishes, to which he could give no name, went crossing each other in his mind. He thought of his dead mother with the bitterest sorrow; but then, again, it seemed to him that what he most longed for was to see that girl again--the one whom he gave the handkerchief to--who had spoken so nicely to him the evening before. And yet he was afraid that if she were to come meeting him out of some street she would turn out to be the old miner in the end. And he was afraid of him; though, at the same time, he would have liked to hear more from him of the wonders of the mine.

"Driven hither and thither by all these fancies, he looked down into the water, and then he thought he saw the silver ripples hardening into the sparkling glimmer in which the grand ships melted away, while the dark clouds, which were beginning to gather and obscure the blue sky, seemed to sink down and thicken into a vault of rock. He was in his dream again, gazing into the immobile face of the majestic woman, and the devouring pain of passionate longing took possession of him as before.

"His shipmates roused him from his reverie to go and join one of their processions, but an unknown voice seemed to whisper in his ear:

"'What are you doing here? Away, away! Your home is in the Mines of Falun. There all the glories which you saw in your dream are waiting for you. Away, away to Falun!'

"For three days Elis hung and loitered about the streets of Goethaborg, constantly haunted by the wonderful imagery of his dream, continually urged by the unknown voice. On the fourth day he was standing at the gate through which the road to Gefle goes, when a tall man walked through it, passing him. Elis fancied he recognized in this man the old miner, and he hastened on after him, but could not overtake him.

"He followed him on and on, without stopping.

"He knew he was on the road to Falun, and this circumstance quieted him in a curious way; for he felt certain that the voice of destiny had spoken to him through the old miner, and that it was he who was now leading him on to his appointed place and fate.

"And, in fact, he many times--particularly if there was any uncertainty about the road--saw the old man suddenly appear out of some ravine, or from thick bushes, or gloomy rocks, stalk away before him, without looking round, and then disappear again.

"At last, after journeying for many weary days, Elis saw, in the distance, two great lakes, with a thick vapour rising between them. As he mounted the hill to westward, he saw some towers and black roofs rising through the smoke. The old man appeared before him, grown to gigantic size, pointed with outstretched hand towards the vapour, and disappeared again amongst the rocks.

"'There lies Falun,' said Elis, 'the end of my journey.'

"He was right; for people, coming up from behind him, said the town of Falun lay between the lakes Runn and Warpann, and that the hill he was ascending was the Guffrisberg, where the main-shaft of the mine was.

"He went bravely on. But when he came to the enormous

gulf, like the jaws of hell itself, the blood curdled in his veins, and he stood as if turned to stone at the sight of this colossal work of destruction.

"The main-shaft of the Falun mines is some twelve hundred feet long, six hundred feet broad, and a hundred and eighty feet deep. Its dark brown sides go, at first for the most part, perpendicularly down, till about half way they are sloped inwards towards the centre by enormous accumulations of stones and refuse. In these, and on the sides, there peeped out here and there timberings of old shafts, formed of strong shores set close together and strongly rabbeted at the ends, in the way that blockhouses are built. Not a tree, not a blade of grass to be seen in all the bare, blank, crumbling congeries of stony chasms; the pointed, jagged, indented masses of rock tower aloft all round in wonderful forms, often like monstrous animals turned to stone, often like colossal human beings. In the abyss itself lie, in wild confusion--pell-mell stones, slag, and scoria, and an eternal, stupefying sulphury vapour rises from the depths, as if the hell-broth, whose reek poisons and kills all the green gladsomeness of nature, were being brewed down below. One would think this was where Dante went down and saw the Inferno, with all its horror and immitigable pain.

"As Elis looked down into this monstrous abyss, he remembered what an old sailor, one of his shipmates, had told him once. This shipmate of his, at a time when he was down with fever, thought the sea had suddenly all gone dry, and the boundless depths of the abyss had opened under him, so

21

that he saw all the horrible creatures of the deep twining and writing about amongst thousands of extraordinary shells, and groves of coral, in dreadful contortions, till they died, and lay dead, with their mouths all gaping. The old sailor said that to see such a vision meant death, ere long, in the waves; and in fact he did very soon after fall overboard, no one knew exactly how, and was drowned without possibility of rescue. Elis thought of that: for indeed the abyss seemed to him to be a good deal like the bottom of the sea run dry; and the black rocks, and the blue and red slag and scoria, were like horrible monsters shooting out polype-arms at him. Two or three miners happened, just then, to be coming up from work in the mine, and in their dark mining clothes, with their black, grimy faces, they were much like ugly, diabolical creatures of some sort, slowly and painfully crawling, and forcing their way up to the surface.

"Elis felt a shudder of dread go through him, and--what he had never experienced in all his career as a sailor--his head got giddy. Unseen hands seemed to be dragging him down into the abyss.

"He closed his eyes and ran a few steps away from it; and it was not till he began climbing up the Guffrisberg again, far from the shaft, and could look up at the bright, sunny sky, that he quite lost the feeling of terror which had taken possession of him. He breathed freely once more, and cried, from the depths of his heart:

"Lord of my Life! what are the dangers of the sea compared with the horror which dwells in that awful abyss

22

of rock? The storm may rage, the black clouds may come whirling down upon the breaking billows, but the beautiful, glorious sun soon gets the mastery again, and the storm is past. But never does the sun penetrate into these black, gloomy caverns; never a freshening breeze of spring can revive the heart down there. No! I shall not join you, black earthworms that you are! Never could I bring myself to lead that terrible life.'

"He resolved to spend that night in Falun, and set off back to Goethaborg the first thing in the morning.

"When he got to the market-place, he found a crowd of people there. A train of miners with their mine-candles in their hands, and musicians before them, was halted before a handsome house. A tall, slightly-built man, of middle age, came out, looking round him with kindly smiles. It was easy to see, by his frank manner, his open brow, and his bright, dark-blue eyes, that he was a genuine Dalkarl. The miners formed a circle round him, and he shook them each cordially by the hand, saying kindly words to them all.

"Elis learned that this was Pehrson Dahlsjoe, Alderman, and owner of a fine 'Fraelse' at Stora-Kopparberg. 'Fraelse' is the name given in Sweden to landed property leased out for the working of the lodes of copper and silver contained in it. The owners of these lands have shares in the mines and are responsible for their management.

"Elis was told, further, that the Assizes were just over that day, and that then the miners went round in procession to the houses of the aldermen, the chief engineers and the minemasters, and were hospitably entertained.

"When he looked at these fine, handsome fellows, with their kindly, frank faces, he forgot all about the earthworms he had seen coming up the shaft. The healthy gladsomeness which broke out afresh in the whole circle, as if new-fanned by a spring breeze, when Pehrson Dahlsjoe came out, was of a different kidney to the senseless noise and uproar of the sailors' Hoensning. The manner in which these miners enjoyed themselves went straight to the serious Elis's heart. He felt indescribably happy; but he could scarce restrain his tears when some of the young pickmen sang an ancient ditty in praise of the miner's calling, and of the happiness of his lot, to a simple melody which touched his heart and soul.

"When this song was ended, Pehrson Dahlsjoe opened his door, and the miners all went into his house one after another. Elis followed involuntarily, and stood at the threshold, so that he overlooked the spacious floor, where the miners took their places on benches. Then the doors at the side opposite to him opened, and a beautiful young lady, in evening dress, came in. She was in the full glory of the freshest bloom of youth, tall and slight, with dark hair in many curls, and a bodice fastened with rich clasps. The miners all stood up, and a low murmur of pleasure ran through their ranks. "Ulla Dahlsjoe!" they said. "What a blessing Heaven has bestowed on our hearty alderman in her!" Even the oldest miners' eyes sparkled when she gave them her hand in kindly greeting, as she did to them all. Then she brought beautiful silver tankards, filled them with splendid Aehl (such as Falun is famous for), and handed them to the guests with a face beaming with kindness and hospitality.

"When Elis saw her a lightning flash seemed to go through his heart, kindling all the heavenly bliss, the love-longings, the passionate ardour lying hidden and imprisoned there. For it was Ulla Dahlsjoe who had held out the hand of rescue to him in his mysterious dream. He thought he understood, now, the deep significance of that dream, and, forgetting the old miner, praised the stroke of fortune which had brought him to Falun.

"Alas! he felt he was but an unknown, unnoticed stranger, standing there on the doorstep miserable, comfortless, alone--and he wished he had died before he saw Ulla, as he now must perish for love and longing. He could not move his eyes from the beautiful creature, and, as she passed close to him, he pronounced her name in a low, trembling voice. She turned, and saw him standing there with a face as red as fire, unable to utter a syllable. So she went up to him, and said, with a sweet smile:

"'I suppose you are a stranger, friend, as you are dressed as a sailor. Well! why are you standing at the door? Come in and join us.'

"Elis felt as if in the blissful paradise of some happy dream, from which he would presently waken to inexpressible wretchedness. He emptied the tankard which she had given him; and Pehrson Dahlsjoe came up, and, after kindly shaking hands with him, asked him where he came from, and what had brought him to Falun.

"Elis felt the warming power of the noble liquor in his veins, and, looking the hearty Dahlsjoe in the eyes, he felt happy and courageous. He told him he was a sailor's son and had been at sea since his childhood, had just come home from the East Indies and found his mother dead; that he was now alone in the world; that the wild sea life had become altogether distasteful to him; that his keenest inclination led him to a miner's calling, and that he wished to get employment as a miner here in Falun. The latter statement, quite the reverse of his recent determination, escaped him involuntarily; it was as if he could not have said anything else to the alderman, nay as if it were the most ardent desire of his soul, although he had not known it till now, himself.

"Pehrson Dahlsjoe looked at him long and carefully, as if he would read his heart; then he said:

"'I cannot suppose, Elis Froebom, that it is mere thoughtless fickleness and the love of change that lead you to give up the calling you have followed hitherto, nor that you have omitted to maturely weigh and consider all the difficulties and hardships of the miner's life before making up your mind to take to it. It is an old belief with us that the mighty elements with which the miner has to deal, and which he controls so bravely, destroy him unless he strains all his being to keep command of them--if he gives place to other thoughts which weaken that vigour which he has to reserve wholly for his constant conflict with Earth and Fire. But if you have properly tested the sincerity of your inward call, and it has withstood the trial, you are come in a good

26

hour. Workmen are wanted in my part of the mine. If you like, you can stay here with me, from now, and to-morrow the Captain will take you down with him, and show you what to set about.'

"Elis's heart swelled with gladness at this. He thought no more of the terror of the awful, hell-like abyss into which he had looked. The thought that he was going to see Ulla every day, and live under the same roof with her, filled him with rapture and delight. He gave way to the sweetest hopes.

"Pehrson Dahlsjoe told the miners that a young hand had applied for employment, and presented him to them then and there. They all looked approvingly at the well-knit lad, and thought he was quite cut out for a miner, as regarded his light, powerful figure, having no doubt that he would not fail in industry and straightforwardness, either.

"One of the men, well advanced in years, came and shook hands with him cordially, saying he was Head-Captain in Pehrson Dahlsjoe's part of the mine, and would be very glad to give him any help and instruction in his power. Elis had to sit down beside this man, who at once began, over his tankard of Aehl, to describe with much minuteness the sort of work which Elis would have to commence with.

"Elis remembered the old miner whom he had seen at Goethaborg, and, strangely enough, found he was able to repeat nearly all that he had told him.

"'Ay,' cried the Head-Captain. 'Where can you have learned all that? It's most surprising! There can't be a doubt that you will be the finest pickman in the mine in a very short time.'

"Ulla--going backwards and forwards amongst the guests and attending to them--often nodded kindly to Elis, and told him to be sure and enjoy himself. 'You're not a stranger now, you know,' she said, 'but one of the household. You have nothing more to do with the treacherous sea the rich mines of Falun are your home.'

"A heaven of bliss and rapture dawned upon Elis at these words of Ulla's. It was evident that she liked to be near him; and Pehrson Dahlsjoe watched his quiet earnestness of character with manifest approval.

"But Elis's heart beat violently when he stood again by the reeking hell-mouth, and went down the mine with the Captain, in his miner's clothes, with the heavy, iron-shod Dalkarl shoes on his feet. Hot vapours soon threatened to suffocate him; and then, presently, the candles flickered in the cutting draughts of cold air that blew in the lower levels. They went down deeper and deeper, on iron ladders at last scarcely a foot wide; and Elis found that his sailor's adroitness at climbing was not of the slightest service to him there.

"They got to the lowest depths of the mine at last, and the Captain showed him what work he was to set about.

"Elis thought of Ulla. Like some bright angel he saw her hovering over him, and he forgot all the terror of the abyss, and the hardness of the toilsome labour.

"It was clear in all his thoughts that it was only if he devoted himself with all the power of his mind, and with all the exertion which his body would endure, to mining work here with Pehrson Dahlsjoe, that there was any possibility of his fondest hopes being some day realized. Wherefore it came about that he was as good at his work as the most practised hand, in an incredibly short space of time.

"Staunch Pehrson Dahlsjoe got to like this good, industrious lad better and better every day, and often told him plainly that he had found in him one whom he regarded as a dear son, as well as a first-class mine-hand. Also Ulla's regard for him became more and more unmistakeable. Often, when he was going to his work, and there was any prospect of danger, she would enjoin him to be sure to take care of himself, with tears in her eyes. And she would come running to meet him when he came back, and always had the finest of Aehl, or some other refreshment, ready for him. His heart danced for joy one day when Pehrson said to him that as he had brought a good sum of money with him, there could be no doubt that--with his habits of economy and industry--he would soon have a 'Hemmans,' or perhaps even a 'Fraelse'; and then not a mineowner in all Falun would say him nay if he asked for his daughter. Fain would Elis have told him at once how unspeakably he loved Ulla, and how all his hopes of happiness were based upon her. But unconquerable shyness, and the doubt whether Ulla really liked him--though he often thought she did--sealed his lips.

"One day it chanced that Elis was at work in the lowest depths of the mine, shrouded in thick, sulphurous vapour, so that his candle only shed a feeble glimmer, and he could scarcely distinguish the run of the lode. Suddenly he heard-

-as if coming from some still deeper cutting--a knocking resounding, as if somebody was at work with a pick-hammer. As that sort of work was scarcely possible at such a depth, and as he knew nobody was down there that day but himself-- because the Captain had got all the men employed in another part of the mine--this knocking and hammering struck him as strange and uncanny. He stopped working, and listened to the hollow sounds, which seemed to come nearer and nearer. All at once he saw, close by him, a black shadow and--as a keen draught of air blew away the sulphur vapour--the old miner whom he had seen in Goethaborg.

"'Good luck,' he cried, 'good luck to Elis Froebom, down here among the stones! What think you of the life, comrade?'

"Elis would fain have asked in what wonderful way the old man had got into the mine; but he kept striking his hammer on the rocks with such force that the fire-sparks went whirling all round, and the mine rang as if with distant thunder. Then he cried, in a terrible voice:

"'There's a grand run of trap just here; but a scurvy, ignorant scoundrel like you sees nothing in it but a narrow streak of 'Trumm' not worth a beanstalk. Down here you're a sightless mole, and you'll always be a mere abomination to the Metal Prince. You're of no use up above either--trying to get hold of the pure Regulus; which you never will--hey! You want to marry Pehrson Dahlsjoe's daughter; that's what you've taken to mine work for, not from any love of your own for the thing. Mind what you're after, double-face; take care that the Metal Prince, whom you are trying to deceive, doesn't take you and dash you down so that the sharp rocks tear you limb from limb. And Ulla will never be your wife; that much I tell you.'

"Elis's anger was kindled at the old man's insulting words.

"'What are you about,' he cried, 'here in my master, Herr Pehrson Dahlsjoe's shaft, where I am doing my duty, and working as hard at it as I can? Be off out of this the way you came, or we'll see which of us two will dash the other's brains out down here.'

"With which he placed himself in a threatening attitude, and swung his hammer about the old man's ears; who only gave a sneering laugh, and Elis saw with terror how he swarmed up the narrow ladder rungs like a squirrel, and disappeared amongst the black labyrinths of the chasms.

"The young man felt paralyzed in all his limbs; he could not go on with his work, but went up. When the old Head-Captain--who had been busy in another part of the mine-- saw him, he cried:

"'For God's sake, Elis, what has happened to you? You're as pale as death. I suppose it's the sulphur gas; you're not accustomed to it yet. Here, take a drink, my lad; that'll do you good.'

"Elis took a good mouthful of brandy out of the flask which the Head-Captain handed to him; and then, feeling better, told him what had happened down in the mine, as also how he had made the uncanny old miner's acquaintance in Goethaborg.

"The Head-Captain listened silently; then dubiously

shook his head and said:

"'That must have been old Torbern that you met with, Elis; and I see, now, that there really is something in the tales that people tell about him. More than one hundred years ago, there was a miner here of the name of Torbern. He seems to have been one of the first to bring mining into a flourishing condition at Falun here, and in his time the profits far exceeded anything that we know of now. Nobody at that time knew so much about mining as Torbern, who had great scientific skill, and thoroughly understood all the ins and outs of the business. The richest lodes seemed to disclose themselves to him, as if he had been endowed with higher powers peculiar to himself; and as he was a gloomy, meditative man, without wife or child--with no regular home, indeed--and very seldom came up to the surface, it couldn't fail that a story soon went about that he was in compact with the mysterious power which dwells in the bowels of the earth, and fuses the metals. Disregarding Torbern's solemn warnings--for he always prophesied that some calamity would happen as soon as the miners' impulse to work ceased to be sincere love for the marvellous metals and ores--people went on enlarging the excavations more and more for the sake of mere profit, till, on St. John's Day of the year 1678, came the terrible landslip and subsidence which formed our present enormous main-shaft, laying waste the whole of the works, as they were then, in the process. It was only after many months' labour that several of the shafts were, with much difficulty, got into workable order again. Nothing was seen or heard of Torbern. There seemed to be no doubt that he had been at work down below at the time of the catastrophe, so that there could be no question what his fate had been. But not long after, and particularly when the work was beginning to go on better again, the miners said they had seen old Torbern in the mine, and that he had given them valuable advice, and pointed out rich lodes to them. Others had come across him at the top of the main-shaft, walking round it, sometimes lamenting, sometimes shouting in wild anger. Other young fellows have come here in the way you yourself did, saying that an old miner had advised them to take to mining, and shewn them the way to Falun. This always happened when there was a scarcity of hands; very likely it was Torbern's way of helping on the cause. But if it really was he whom you had those words with in the mine, and if he spoke of a fine run of trap, there isn't a doubt that there must be a grand vein of ore thereabouts, and we must see, to-morrow, if we can come across it. Of course you remember that we call rich veins of the kind "trap-runs," and that a "Trumm" is a vein which goes sub-dividing into several smaller ones, and probably gets lost altogether.'

"When Elis, tossed hither and thither by various thoughts, went into Pehrson Dahlsjoe's, Ulla did not come meeting him as usual. She was sitting with downcast looks, and--as he thought--eyes which had been weeping; and beside her was a handsome young fellow, holding her hand, and trying to say all sorts of kind and amusing things, to which she seemed to pay little attention. Pehrson Dahlsjoe took Elis--who, seized by gloomy presentiments, was keeping a darksome glance riveted on the pair--into another room, and said:

"Well, Elis, you will soon have it in your power to give me a proof of your regard and sincerity. I have always looked upon you as a son, but you will soon take the place of one altogether. The man whom you see in there is a well-to-do merchant, Eric Olavsen by name, from Goethaborg. I am giving him my daughter for his wife, at his desire. He will take her to Goethaborg, and then you will be left alone with me, my only support in my declining years. Well, you say nothing? You turn pale? I trust this step doesn't displease you, and that now that I'm going to lose my daughter you are not going to leave me too? But I hear Olavsen mentioning my name; I must go in.'

"With which he went back to the room.

"Elis felt a thousand red-hot irons tearing at his heart. He could find no words, no tears. In wild despair he ran out, out of the house, away to the great mine-shrift.

"That monstrous chasm had a terrible appearance by day; but now, when night had fallen, and the moon was just peeping down into it, the desolate crags looked like a numberless horde of horrible monsters, the direful brood of hell, rolling and writhing, in wildest confusion, all about its reeking sides and clefts, and flashing up fiery eyes, and shooting forth glowing claws to clutch the race of mortals.

"Torbern, Torbern,' Elis cried, in a terrible voice, which made the rocks re-echo. 'Torbern, I am here; you were not wrong I was a wretched fool to fix my hopes on any earthly love, up on the surface here. My treasure, and my life, my all-in-all, are down below. Torbern! take me down with you! Show me the richest veins, the lodes of ore, the glowing metal! I will dig and bore, and toil and labour. Never, never more will I come back to see the light of day. Torbern! Torbern! take me down to you!'

"He took his flint and steel from his pocket, lighted his candle, and went quickly down the shaft, into the deep cutting where he had been on the previous day, without seeing anything of the old man. But what was his amazement when, at the deepest point, he saw the vein of metal with the utmost clearness and distinctness, so that he could trace every one of its ramifications, and its risings and fallings. But as he kept his gaze fixed more and more firmly on this wonderful vein, a dazzling light seemed to come shining through the shaft, and the walls of rock grew transparent as crystal. That mysterious dream which he had had in Goethaborg came back upon him. He was looking upon those Elysian Fields of glorious metallic trees and plants, on which, by way of fruits, buds, and blossoms, hung jewels streaming with fire. He saw the maidens, and he looked upon the face of the mighty queen. She put out her arms, drew him to her, and pressed him to her breast, Then a burning ray darted through his heart, and all his consciousness was merged in a feeling of floating in waves of some blue, transparent, glittering mist.

"'Elis Froebom! Elis Froebom!' a powerful voice from above cried out, and the reflection of torches began shining in the shaft. It was Pehrson Dahlsjoe come down with the

Captain to search for the lad, who had been seen running in the direction of the main-shaft like a mad creature.

"They found him standing as if turned to stone, with his face pressed against the cold, hard rock.

"'What are you doing down here in the night-time, you foolish fellow?' cried Pehrson. 'Pull yourself together, and come up with us. Who knows what good news you may hear.'

"Elis went up in profound silence after Dahlsjoe, who did not cease to rate him soundly for exposing himself to such danger. It was broad daylight in the morning when they got to the house.

"Ulla threw herself into Elis's arms with a great cry, and called him by the fondest names, and Pehrson said to him:

"'You foolish fellow! How could I help seeing, long ago, that you were in love with Ulla, and that it was on her account, in all probability, that you were working so hard in the mine? Neither could I help seeing that she was just as fond of you. Could I wish for a better son-in-law than a fine, hearty, hard-working, honest miner--than just yourself, Elis? What vexed me was that you never would speak.'

"'We scarcely knew ourselves,' said Ulla, 'how fond we were of each other.'

"'However that may be,' said Pehrson, 'I was annoyed that Elis didn't tell me openly and candidly of his love for you, and that was why I made up the story about Eric Olavsen, which was so nearly being the death of you, you silly fellow. Not but what I wished to try you, Ulla, into the bargain. Eric Olavsen has been married for many a day, and I give my daughter to you, Elis Froebom, for, I say it again, I couldn't wish for a better son-in-law.'

"Tears of joy and happiness ran down Elis's cheeks. The highest bliss which his imagination had pictured had come to pass so suddenly and unexpectedly that he could scarce believe it was anything but another blissful dream. The workpeople came to dinner, by Dahlsjoe's invitation, in honour of the event. Ulla had dressed in her prettiest attire, and looked more charming than ever, so that they all cried, over and over again, 'Ey! what a sweet and charming creature Elis has got for a betrothed! May God bless them and make them happy!'

"Yet the terror of the past night still lay upon Elis's pale face, and he often stared about him as if he were far away from all that was going on round him. 'Elis, darling, what is the matter?' Ulla asked anxiously. He pressed her to his heart and said, 'Yes, yes, you are my own, and all is well.' But in the midst of all his happiness he often felt as though an icy hand clutched at his heart, and a dismal voice asked him,

"Is it your highest ideal, then, to be betrothed to Ulla? Wretched fool! Have you not looked upon the face of the queen?'

"He felt himself overpowered by an indescribable, anxious alarm. He was haunted and tortured by the thought that one of the workmen would suddenly assume gigantic proportions, and to his horror he would recognize in him Torbern, come to remind him, in a terrible manner, of the subterranean realm of gems and metals to which he had devoted himself.

"And yet he could see no reason why the spectral old man should be hostile to him, or what connection there was between his mining work and his love.

"Pehrson, seeing Elis's disordered condition, attributed it to the trouble he had gone through, and his nocturnal visit to the mine. Not so, Ulla, who, seized by a secret presentiment, implored her lover to tell her what terrible thing had happened to him to tear him away from her so entirely. This almost broke his heart. It was in vain that he tried to tell her of the wonderful face which had revealed itself to him in the depths of the mine. Some unknown power seemed to seal his lips forcibly; he felt as though the terrible face of the queen were looking out from his heart, so that if he mentioned her everything about him would turn to stone, to dark, black rock, as at the sight of the Medusa's frightful head. All the glory and magnificence which had filled him with rapture in the abyss appeared to him now as a pandemonium of immitigable torture, deceptively decked out to allure him to his ruin.

"Dahlsjoe told him he must stay at home for a few days, so as to shake off the sickness which he seemed to have fallen into. And during this time Ulla's affection, which now streamed bright and clear from her candid, child-like heart, drove away the memory of his fateful adventure in the mine-depths. Joy and happiness brought him back to life, and to belief in his good fortune, and in the impossibility of its being ever interfered with by any evil power.

"When he went down the pit again, everything appeared quite different to what it used to be. The most glorious veins lay clear and distinct before his eyes. He worked twice as zealously as before; he forgot everything else. When he got to the surface again, it cost him an effort of thought to remember about Pehrson Dahlsjoe, about his Ulla, even. He felt as if divided into two halves, as if his better self, his real personality, went down to the central point of the earth, and there rested in bliss in the queen's arms, whilst he went to his darksome dwelling in Falun. When Ulla spoke of their love, and the happiness of their future life together, he would begin to talk of the splendours of the depths, and the inestimably precious treasures that lay hidden there, and in so doing would get entangled in such wonderful, incomprehensible sayings, that alarm and terrible anxiety took possession of the poor child, who could not divine why Elis should be so completely altered from his former self. He kept telling the Captain, and Dahlsjoe himself, with the greatest delight, that he had discovered the richest veins and the most magnificent trap-runs, and when these turned out to be nothing but unproductive rock, he would laugh contemptuously and say that none but he understood the secret signs, the significant writing, fraught with hidden meaning, which the queen's own hand had inscribed on the rocks, and that it was sufficient to understand those signs without bringing to light what they indicated.

"The old Captain looked sorrowfully at Elis, who spoke, with wild gleaming eyes, of the glorious paradise which glowed down in the depths of the earth. 'That terrible old Torbern has been at him,' he whispered in Dahlsjoe's ear.

"'Pshaw! don't believe these miners' yarns,' cried Dahlsjoe. 'He's a deep-thinking serious fellow, and love has turned his head, that's all. Wait till the marriage is over, then we'll hear no more of the trap-runs, the treasures, and the subterranean paradise.'

"The wedding-day, fixed by Dahlsjoe, came at last. For a few days previously Elis had been more tranquil, more serious, more sunk in deep reflection than ever. But, on the other hand, never had he shown such affection for Ulla as at this time. He could not leave her for a moment, and never went down the mine at all. He seemed to have forgotten his restless excitement about mining work, and never a word of the subterranean kingdom crossed his lips. Ulla was all rapture. Her fear lest the dangerous powers of the subterranean world, of which she had heard old miners speak, had been luring him to his destruction, had left her; and Dahlsjoe, too, said, laughing to the Captain, 'You see, Elis was only a little light-headed for love of my Ulla.'

"Early on the morning of the wedding-day, which was St. John's Day as it chanced, Elis knocked at the door of Ulla's room. She opened it, and started back terrified at the sight of Elis, dressed in his wedding clothes already, deadly pale, with dark gloomy fire sparkling in his eyes.

"'I only want to tell you, my beloved Ulla,' he said, in a faint, trembling voice, 'that we are just arrived at the summit of the highest good fortune which it is possible for mortals to attain. Everything has been revealed to me in the night which is just over. Down in the depths below, hidden in chlorite and mica, lies the cherry-coloured sparkling almandine, on which the tablet of our lives is graven. I have to give it to you as a wedding present. It is more splendid than the most glorious blood-red carbuncle, and when, united in truest affection, we look into its streaming splendour together, we shall see and understand the peculiar manner in which our hearts and souls have grown together into the wonderful branch which shoots from the queen's heart, at the central point of the globe. All that is necessary is that I go and bring this stone to the surface, and that I will do now, as fast as I can. Take care of yourself meanwhile, beloved darling. I will be back to you directly.'

"Ulla implored him, with bitter tears, to give up all idea of such a dream-like undertaking, for she felt a strong presentiment of disaster; but Elis declared that without this stone he should never know a moment's peace or happiness, and that there was not the slightest danger of any kind. He pressed her fondly to his heart, and was gone.

"The guests were all assembled to accompany the bridal pair to the church of Copparberg, where they were to be married, and a crowd of girls, who were to be the bridesmaids and walk in procession before the bride (as is the custom of the place), were laughing and playing round Ulla. The musicians were tuning their instruments to begin a wedding march. It was almost noon, but Elis had not made his appearance. Suddenly some miners came running up, horror in their pale faces, with the news that there had been a terrible catastrophe, a subsidence of the earth, which had destroyed the whole of Pehrson Dahlsjoe's part of the mine.

"'Elis! oh, Elis! you are gone!' screamed Ulla, wildly, and fell as if dead. Then only, for the first time, Dahlsjoe learned from the Captain that Elis had gone down the main-shaft in the morning. Nobody else had been in the mine, the rest of the men having been invited to the wedding. Dahlsjoe and all the others hurried off to search, at the imminent danger of their own lives. In vain! Elis Froebom was not to be found. There could be no question that the earth-fall had buried him in the rock. And thus came desolation and mourning upon the house of brave Pehrson Dahlsjoe, at the moment when he thought he was assured of peace and happiness for the remainder of his days.

"Long had stout Pehrson Dahlsjoe been dead, his daughter Ulla long lost sight of and forgotten. Nobody in Falun remembered them. More than fifty years had gone by since Froebom's luckless wedding-day, when it chanced that some miners who were making a connection-passage between two shafts, found, at a depth of three hundred yards, buried in vitriolated water, the body of a young miner, which seemed, when they brought it to the daylight, to be turned to stone.

"The young man looked as if he were lying in a deep sleep, so perfectly preserved were the features of his lace, so wholly without trace of decay his new suit of miner's clothes, and even the flowers in his breast. The people of the neighbourhood all collected round the young man, but no one recognized him or could say who he had been, and none of the workmen missed any comrade.

"The body was going to be taken to Falun, when out of the distance an old, old woman came creeping slowly and painfully up on crutches.

"Here's the old St. John's Day grandmother!' the miners said. They had given her this name because they had noticed that she came always every year on St. John's Day up to the main shaft, and looked down into its depths, weeping, lamenting, and wringing her hands as she crept round it, then going away again.

"The moment she saw the body she threw away her crutches, lifted her arms to Heaven, and cried, in the most heartrending accents of the deepest lamentation:

"'Oh! Elis Froebom! Oh, my sweet, sweet bridegroom!'

"And she cowered down beside the body, took the stony hands and pressed them to her heart, chilled with age, but throbbing still with the fondest love, like some naphtha flame under the surface ice.

"'Ah!' she said, looking round at the spectators, 'nobody, nobody among you all, remembers poor Ulla Dahlsjoe, this poor boy's happy bride fifty long years ago. When I went away, in my terrible sorrow and despair, to Ornaes, old Torbern comforted me, and told me I should see my poor Elis, who was buried in the rock upon our wedding-day, yet once more here upon earth. And I have come every year and looked for him, all longing and faithful love. And now this blessed meeting has been granted me this day. Oh, Elis! Elis! my beloved husband!'

"She wound her arms about him as if she would never part from him more, and the people all stood round in the deepest emotion.

"Fainter and fainter grew her sobs and sighs, till they ceased to be audible.

"The miners closed round. They would have raised poor Ulla, but she had breathed out her life upon her bridegroom's body. The spectators noticed now that it was beginning to crumble into dust. The appearance of petrifaction had been deceptive.

"In the church of Copparberg, where they were to have been married fifty years before, they laid in the earth the ashes of Elis Froebom, and with them the body of her who had been thus 'Faithful unto death.'"

"I see," said Theodore, when he had finished, and the friends sat looking straight before them in silence, "that you don't much like this story of mine. Perhaps, in your present mood of mind, it strikes you as too painful."

"It does produce a terribly melancholy effect upon one," said Ottmar, "and, to speak my candid opinion, I cannot say that I care about all the Swedish 'Fraelse' holders, the national festivities, the spectral miners, visions, and so forth. The simple account in Schubert's 'Night Side of Natural Science,' of the finding of a body in the Falun Mine, which an old woman recognized as her betrothed of fifty years before, affected me much more deeply."

"I must betake myself for aid to our patron, Serapion," said Theodore; "for the story of the miner really came to my fancy exactly as I have told it."

"Everybody has his own way of looking at things," said Lothair, "but perhaps it is as well that it was to us that you read this tale, inasmuch as we have all some knowledge of mining matters, of Falun, and of Swedish manners and customs. Other people might say you had sometimes been a little unintelligible from the use of too much mining phraseology; and it isn't everybody who would know that the 'Aehl' which you mention so often is simply a fine, strong sort of beer."

"Theodore's story has not displeased me so much as it has you, Ottmar," said Cyprian. "Writers very often show us people who perish in some disastrous way as having been at issue with themselves all through their lives, as if under the control of unknown powers of darkness. This is what Theodore has done; and I must say I approve of it, because I think it is exceedingly true to nature. I have known people who have suddenly seemed to alter and change completely--who have appeared to be suddenly petrified (so to speak) within themselves, or driven hither and thither by hostile powers, in constant unrest, till some fearful catastrophe has withdrawn them from life."

"Stop, stop!" cried Lothair. "If we give this spirit-seer Cyprian a chance, we shall be drawn into a regular labyrinth of dreams, presentiments, and all the rest of it. Allow me to dispel the gloomy tone which has come upon us at one stroke, by reading you--as a finale to our present sitting--a children's story which I wrote a short time ago, as I believe, under the direct inspiration of the tricksy spirit Puck, himself."

"A children's story by you, Lothair!" they all cried.

"Even so," said Lothair. "It may seem to you a piece of insanity that I should write a children's story; but let me read it to you, and then give your verdicts."

Lothair took a carefully written MS. from his pocket, and read:--

www.ingramcontent.com/pod-product-compliance
Lightning Source LLC
Chambersburg PA
CBHW030531260626
47157CB00005B/1973

* 9 7 8 1 4 4 7 4 6 5 6 1 4 *